The Shoebox Kids

The M Combination Mystery

Written by
Eric Stoffle

Book 4
Created by
Jerry D. Thomas

Pacific Press Publishing Association
Boise, Idaho
Oshawa, Ontario, Canada

Edited by Jerry D. Thomas
Designed by Dennis Ferree
Cover art by Stephanie Britt
Illustrations by Mark Ford
Typeset in New Century Schoolbook 14/17

Copyright © 1996 by
Pacific Press Publishing Association
Printed in the United States of America
All Rights Reserved

Library of Congress Cataloging-in-Publication
Data:

Stoffle, Eric D., 1963-
    The missing combination mystery / written by Eric D.
Stoffle.
        p.   cm. — (The shobox kids ; 4)
    Summary: When Christ finds an old safe in his grand-
parents' basement, he and his friends begin a hunt for the
missing combination that leads to a revelation about the
donor of the cross on the hill overlooking Mill Valley.
    ISBN 0-8163-1276-1 (alk. paper)
    [1. Safes. 2. Christian life. 3. Mystery and detective
stories.]   I. Title. II. Series.
PZ7.S8698Mi   1996
[Fic]—dc20   95-50445
                                                     CIP
                                                      AC

96 97 98 99 00 • 5 4 3 2 1

Contents

Other Books in The Shoebox Kids Series

Hi!

Do you ever feel left out, like your friends want to be with someone else instead of you? What if you really needed those friends to help you solve a mystery?

The Shoebox Kids are in the middle of another mysterious problem. In their fourth book, Chris and Maria discover an old safe in their grandparents' basement. But no one knows the combination!

The Mystery of the Missing Combination is written by my friend, Eric Stoffle. He created a story that will keep you guessing! Who gave the money to build the cross above Mill Valley? Chris and Maria think the answer is inside the old safe. As they follow the clues, Chris learns some important lessons about friendship and jealousy—and about being a Christian.

That's what the Shoebox Kids books are really all about—learning to be a Christian, not just at church, but at home and at school and on the playground. If you're trying to be a friend of Jesus, then the Shoebox Kids books are just what you're looking for!

Can you figure out where the missing combination is before Chris and Maria do?

Jerry D. Thomas

P.S. Coming soon—*The Broken Dozen Mystery!*

CHAPTER

1

Secret in the Basement

Chris tiptoed down the steps to his grandma's basement. He glanced back several times to make sure he wasn't being followed. And to make sure no one was peeking through the crack by the door to see where he was going.

At the bottom of the stairs, Chris checked out the area underneath the steps. It was dark under there, all right, but that was the first place they would look. He had to find a really good place to hide—a place where no one would ever find him. *I'm glad only one of the lights works*, he thought. *The long shadows will help hide me.*

7

As he looked around the rest of the basement, Chris shook his head. *There's so much stuff here.* A bed frame and mattresses were leaning up against a far wall. He thought about crawling behind the box springs to hide. *There are too many cobwebs*, he decided with a shiver, *and that means spiders.*

Chris glanced at his watch. He was running out of time! He stepped between old bike parts, folding chairs, and exercise equipment. An old console television sat in a far, dark corner of the basement. *Maybe I could hide behind that*, Chris thought. At his next step, a cobweb wrapped across his face.

"Eeuw," Chris said, brushing it off his face. "Pooh! Phooey." The sticky web kept hanging on as he shook his hand. "That's disgusting!" he whispered to himself.

Suddenly, the door at the top of the stairs creaked opened! Chris slipped quietly in behind the television and held his breath. He heard footsteps coming down the stairs. Then they stopped.

"Chwis . . . ? Where are you, Chwis?"

"Shhh, Yoyo," Maria whispered. "We want Chris to think he's fooled us. Then he might give away his hiding place."

"OK."

Chris heard Yoyo's whisper and smiled to himself. Maria and Yoyo would never think to look for him so far back in the basement. The shadows were a little scary, but it was worth it if Maria and Yoyo gave up looking for him. Then he would win their game of hide-and-seek.

Something tickled Chris's arm. Whatever it was started moving. It moved really fast, then stopped. Chris felt a chill climb up his spine and go right into his hair, making it stand on end.

"Aagh!" he cried, jumping out of his hiding place. "I hate spiders!"

Yoyo screamed and hugged Maria with both arms.

Chris jumped around in circles, swinging his arms wildly to brush himself off. He looked as if he were doing some sort of Indian war dance.

Maria patted Yoyo's head. Then she folded her arms. "Chris, you should know better than to scare Yoyo!" she criticized.

When Chris finally stopped dancing around, he frowned at Maria. "I wasn't trying to scare you or Yoyo. I thought I had a spider on me. I was trying to get it off." He knelt down beside Yoyo.

"I'm sorry if I scared you, Yoyo," he apologized.

"OK, Chwis. I'm glad it was you." Yoyo gave Chris a big hug. Suddenly her eyes got big and round. "What's that, Chwis?" she asked, pointing at something that looked like a big metal box partially covered by a blanket. The blanket had been covering the box until Chris had knocked it off with his spider dance.

Chris turned around. "I don't know, Yoyo. Let's look."

Maria folded the blanket off the metal box. "It sure is big," she said. "What is it for?"

Chris knelt down. He tried to nudge the box, but it wouldn't budge. "Wow. It's heavy too!"

Maria uncovered it all the way. "Look, there's a dial on the back, Chris."

Chris checked it out. "That's the front, Maria," he said. Grinning, he looked from Maria to Yoyo. "This is an old, old safe. I wonder whose it is?"

"Probably Grandma and Grandpa's," Maria said.

"Let's go ask," Chris suggested, heading for the stairs.

Maria ran over and got in front of him. "Wait a second, brother. Come here, Yoyo," she called.

Yoyo came over and stood beside her sister.

She stood at attention with her hand in Maria's.

"You can't go back upstairs until you say we won the game," Maria told Chris. "Right, Yoyo?"

"Wight," Yoyo agreed.

"OK, you two win the game this time," Chris agreed. "Now let's go up and ask about the safe!"

Chris, Maria, and Yoyo all burst into the kitchen, where Grandma was putting supper on the table. "Good," Grandma said. "Now I won't have to go call you to come and eat. You're already here."

Chris glanced at the vegetable soup and crackers and sandwiches. They looked really good, but suddenly he wasn't hungry anymore. He started to ask about the safe. "Grandma—"

"Will you get some glasses out of the cupboard, Chris?" Grandma interrupted. "Yoyo, we need the milk out of the refrigerator, please."

Yoyo skipped over and got the milk while Chris reached for the glasses. He almost got five. Then he remembered Grandpa would be gone for the evening because he was visiting a sick friend in the hospital.

"This is great!" Maria said as she sat down at the table. "I'm glad we get to stay over here when Mom and Dad go out on dates."

Yoyo pulled herself up into her chair. "Me too."

Chris set the glasses down and poured Yoyo some milk. He handed the milk to Maria, and she poured her own. Chris started to ask about the safe again. "Grandma—"

"Let's bow our heads for a blessing on the food," Grandma said.

Grandma asked the blessing. When everyone's eyes opened, Maria started talking. "Grandma, what's that old safe down in the basement used for?"

Grandma's face went blank for a moment. "What old—?" she started to ask. But then her eyes lighted up when she remembered. "I'd almost forgotten that was down there. You must mean my father's old safe, your great-grandpa's."

"Is that whose it is?" Chris asked. "It must be real old."

Grandma nodded. "When your great-grandpa died, we brought it over here and stored it in the basement. It took several men to get it down those stairs. I don't know how we'll ever move it again."

"Do you store valuable stuff in there?" Maria asked.

Grandma smiled. "No, honey, Grandpa and I don't store anything in that old safe. We don't know the combination, and it would cost a lot of money to have a locksmith open it. Your great-grandpa didn't leave anything valuable in that safe, anyway."

"How do you know?" Chris asked. He watched Grandma take a bite of bread.

"Well, Chris, I guess I don't know for sure that there's nothing in there. But before your great-grandpa died he kept his important papers and possessions in a safe-deposit box down at the bank."

Chris barely touched his soup. He was too excited. Already his mind was leaping ahead, imagining what might be hidden in that old safe. "Maybe Great-Grandpa wrote down the combination somewhere," he said. "Somewhere where we can find it."

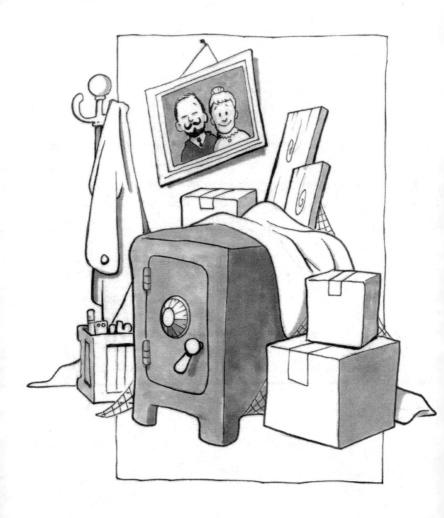

2

The Missing Combination

"Who's Great-Grampa?" Yoyo sputtered with soup in her mouth. "Who's Great-Grampa?"

Grandma gently wiped Yoyo's mouth. "When you have finished your supper, Yoyo, I'll show you some pictures of Great-Grandpa Archer." Grandma looked at Chris and Maria. "I've looked through all your great-grandpa's things. All his papers. I didn't see anything that might be a combination," Grandma said.

Chris and Maria sighed, feeling let down. Chris felt sure there was something valuable inside that old safe. "Maybe Great-Grandpa put some money in there or gold or something," he said.

Grandma shook her head. "If I thought there was anything of value in that old safe, I would have had it opened years ago. But if you kids would like to look for the combination, those boxes sitting beside the safe have a lot of your great-grandpa's things in them."

Chris's eyes lighted up. "Can we look?"

Grandma smiled. "Yes, you may. But only after you eat. Yoyo and I will go into the living room and look at the photo album while you're looking for clues."

Chris cleaned up his bowl of soup in a flash. Maria was right behind him when he headed for the door leading downstairs. Grandma had mentioned the word *clues*. He and Maria *would* be looking for clues, just like real detectives.

"Wait," Maria said. "Maybe we should get a flashlight. Remember, that light bulb over the safe has burned out."

"Good idea," Chris agreed.

When they returned, Maria pulled the safe's blanket all the way off while Chris uncovered the boxes Grandma had said held some of Great-Grandpa's things.

"I feel weird looking at these things," Maria said when she knelt down to look in the boxes with Chris. "Great-Grandpa died a long time ago. He never even knew us."

Chris nodded solemnly. "I wish I could have known him. Mom says he wrote lots of important books." He examined an old camera and set it on the floor beside him. Then he picked out an old pair of glasses. The metal was tarnished, and one of the earpieces was loose. "Look at these old things. Do you suppose Great-Grandpa Archer used these when he wrote?"

Chris handed the glasses to Maria, and she turned them over in her hands again and again. "I think he did," Maria said. "You know what? I feel like I know Great-Grandpa better already."

"Here's an old dictionary." Chris held up a book with the cover about ready to fall off.

"What's this!" Maria said excitedly, pulling out some pictures held together with a rubber band. The rubber band was so old and brittle it broke when she tried to take it off. Time had even made the pictures a little bit yellow and faded.

Scooting around next to Maria, Chris looked at the pictures with her.

17

"I think he looked better without a beard than with one," Maria said.

"Let me see," Chris muttered. He flipped through the pictures. "I don't see anywhere where he's not wearing a beard."

"Not in any of those! But I saw a picture of him somewhere, and he wasn't wearing a beard in it," Maria stated.

Chris looked at his sister suspiciously. He had never seen such a picture. "Where did you see a picture like that?"

Maria shrugged. "I don't remember. I must have seen it when I was real little."

"Oh, well, it doesn't matter, I guess." Chris pulled some more items out of the box. He found a big round cookie tin with a lid on it. Jiggling it, he discovered something rattling around inside. After prying at the lid for several seconds, he finally got it off.

"What'd you find?" Maria asked.

Chris stared inside the tin without speaking. "Wow! Look at this! I know I've seen this somewhere before." He held up a wooden figurine that stood about ten inches tall and was drawing an arrow.

"It just looks like some old Indian shooting

an arrow," Maria said. "We're supposed to be looking for the combination to the safe. Remember?"

"It's not an Indian," Chris stated. "I think it's a soldier, like those guys hundreds of years ago in England. See, he's wearing mail armor."

Maria shrugged. "I don't care."

Suddenly a huge shadow fell across Maria and Chris and the safe.

Neither Grandma nor Yoyo would cast a shadow that big! Chris thought. He couldn't make himself turn to see who it was. He noticed that Maria's eyes were big and round, as if she had just seen a ghost.

"What are you two doing down here?" a big voice boomed.

Chris had heard that voice before. Every weekend, as a matter of fact! He spun around and looked up. "Whew. What are you doing down here, Pastor Hill?"

"Your grandmother said you were down here going through some things. I thought I would come down and say Hi before I left. I just dropped by to tell her that the city of Mill Valley is planning a fiftieth-anniversary celebration this Easter weekend to commemorate the building of the cross that stands on the hill above town."

"I didn't know that cross was so old," Maria said.

"Neither did I," Chris added.

Pastor Hill knelt down. "To tell you the truth, neither did I until the mayor called me about the celebration. It's a great idea, but no one seems to know who donated it. One thing the mayor wanted to do is have a special award for the person who donated the money to build the cross. Be sure and tell your parents about it too," he said.

When Pastor Hill left, Maria turned slowly back to Chris. Her eyes were sparkling, but her face was almost white. She was excited and worried at the same time. "Ch—Chris, I—I think I know who donated the money to build the cross. I think it was Great-Grandpa Archer!"

3

The Cross on the Hill

"What makes you think Great-Grandpa donated that money?" Chris asked, staring at his sister. "We've only found these few things, and nothing that says Great-Grandpa Archer had anything to do with the cross."

Chris could tell Maria was getting really excited about something. She stood up and paced back and forth, thinking hard. "I just know he did. But how can we prove it? I wish I could remember," she muttered.

"Remember what?" Chris asked. He was sitting cross-legged on the floor, with the wooden statue in his lap.

"I wish I could remember where I saw that picture of Great-Grandpa without a beard."

Chris shook his head. "That won't help us any."

Maria dropped down on her knees in front of Chris. "It might help. I remember that he was standing beside the cross. Maybe there's a clue in the picture. We'll just have to find it. Even if there isn't a clue in the picture, if the picture was taken fifty years ago, that would prove something. That would be about the same time the cross was built."

Chris finally agreed. "If you say you saw that picture, I believe you. After all, it's our only clue."

Keeping out the statue Chris had found and Maria's handful of pictures of Great-Grandpa, they quickly repacked everything they had taken out of the boxes.

Grandma was just putting her photo albums back in the cupboard when Chris and Maria got upstairs. Grandma put her finger in front of her lips and pointed toward the sofa. Yoyo was asleep, so Maria tiptoed into the living room and whispered to Grandma. "Can I look at those photo albums before you put them away, Grandma?"

"Yes, dear. Did you find anything interesting downstairs?"

Maria nodded. She gave Chris one album, and she took the other two. Then they went into the kitchen. "I found these old pictures," she told Grandma, pointing at the handful she had brought up from downstairs and set on the table.

"And I found this, Grandma," Chris said, holding out the statue.

"Oh yes!" Grandma exclaimed. "A friend of your great-grandpa's carved that for him many, many years ago. I had forgotten all about it. Your Great-Grandpa Archer was proud of his name, and that's why his friend thought of carving an archer. A long time ago in Europe, people didn't have last names. Then people started using the name of their occupation. That's how names like Mason and Baker and Archer came to be in use," Grandma explained.

Chris carefully set the archer on the counter. "It sure is neat," he said in a whisper.

Grandma smiled. She was watching the expression on Chris's face. "You may keep it if you wish," she said. "Of course, you would have to take special care of it. I'm sure your great-grandpa would have wanted you to have it."

Chris was thrilled. "I'll take very good care of it, Grandma. Thank you."

"And you may keep those pictures you found, Maria. And, kids, you're welcome to go through that stuff down in the basement anytime, but don't take anything unless you ask permission first. OK?"

Maria and Chris nodded in agreement.

"Now what are you two looking for?" Grandma asked. She went around the table and stood behind Maria. Chris joined her.

"Well," Maria said, "I thought I remembered a picture of Great-Grandpa where he wasn't wearing a beard. He was standing beside the cross up on the hill, the one Pastor Hill told us the town is planning to have an anniversary celebration for."

"Oh yes. The pastor told me about it. I wonder who donated the money to build it?"

Maria glanced sternly at Chris out of the corner of her eye. Chris knew she was trying to tell him not to say anything. And he wasn't going to breathe a word of it to anyone, either.

At least not until they had more proof.

"I suppose Pastor Hill's talking about the cross made you remember the picture you are looking for," Grandma said. She went over to the stove and turned on the rear burner under the teakettle. "Would you like some hot chocolate?"

"Yes," Chris said. "Please."

"Thank you, Grandma," Maria said. Then, when Grandma turned around, she waved for Chris to sit down beside her. "You look through that album," she told him.

Chris pulled the photo album to him and opened it up. He studied each and every picture. There were hundreds of them, he guessed. Maria finished looking through her first album and opened another one. By the time Chris closed his album, the teakettle was whistling. He waited for Grandma to shut it off, but she never came into the kitchen. Finally, he went over and turned it off himself. He stood there for a minute, looking around.

"What's the matter, Chris?" Maria asked.

"Notice how dark it's gotten?" Chris said.

Maria looked around as if she hadn't noticed anything but the photo albums in the past fifteen minutes. "So?"

"And where is Grandma? She didn't even hear the teakettle whistling."

Maria scooted her chair back and stood up. She pointed toward the counter. "And she's not the only one that's missing!"

Chris look at the counter, right at the spot Maria was pointing. "My statue! It's gone!"

Chris searched everywhere in the kitchen. Maria even helped some. But a quick search told them the statue was nowhere to be found. "What could have happened to it?" Chris asked, stomping his foot. "It was right here just a minute ago."

"I don't know," Maria said. "And where is Grandma?"

Chris shrugged again. "She must be in the house somewhere."

"Well, if she were in the house, I don't think she would have left the teakettle whistling like that," Maria said.

Going to the back door, Chris opened it and looked around the backyard. "She's not out here." When he got back to the kitchen, he shook his head. "I don't know where she went."

"Let's check on Yoyo," Maria suggested. She

and Chris went into the living room and found Yoyo still asleep on the sofa. But no Grandma. "I don't believe she just disappeared," Maria said.

"I don't think so, either," Chris murmured. "Let me check down the hall." He checked Grandma and Grandpa's bedroom and the spare room. Maria was waiting on the sofa beside Yoyo when he got back. "She's not in the house anywhere," he told Maria.

Maria looked worried. "This is scary," she said.

Suddenly something banged against the front door, and Chris nearly jumped out of his shoes.

"See what it is," Maria told him.

Chris gave her a doubtful look. "I—I don't . . . know . . ." He let out a breath of air and started forward. When he got to the door, he turned the handle slowly and opened it an inch at a time. Then he threw the door open all the way and jumped outside.

"Let me help you, Grandma," he said, reaching for the big box she was trying to get through the screen door.

"Thank you, Chris. I was hoping to be able to bring this box of clothes inside by myself. I guess I'm not as strong as I used to be."

After the box was inside, Grandma sat down to rest. "Whew," she said. "Mrs. Williams sure had a load of clothes for community services."

Maria let out a long sigh of relief herself. "We thought you had disappeared, Grandma."

"Oh no. I just stepped out for a minute to speak to Mrs. Williams and bring in this box of clothes. I think your imaginations must be working overtime."

"Huh, uh, Grandma," Chris argued. "What about my statue? My statue is missing! Come here. I'll show you!"

Grandma went into the kitchen with Chris.

"It was right here," Chris said. "On the countertop. Now it's gone!" Chris pointed at the countertop.

4

Searching for Clues

The empty countertop didn't bother Grandma at all. "The statue isn't missing, Chris. I put it in your backpack before I went outside so you wouldn't forget it. I didn't want it to get knocked onto the floor accidentally. You two were concentrating on the photo albums and didn't notice what I was doing. Or that I left," Grandma explained.

Chris's face turned red. *I guess it was pretty foolish of us to get so upset when we couldn't find Grandma or the statue,* he thought.

"Maria, did you find what you were looking for in the photo albums?" Grandma asked.

Maria shook her head. "No. I thought I remembered a picture of Great-Grandpa Archer when he wasn't wearing a beard. Chris didn't believe me. I thought it was a picture of him standing by the cross Pastor Hill was talking about."

Grandma sat down at the table. "Let me think. Now that you mention it, I do remember a time when Dad shaved his beard off. It was many, many years ago, and he let it grow right back. He always liked a beard."

"Do you remember the picture, Grandma?" Maria asked hopefully.

"If there is such a picture, I don't remember it, Maria. I'm sorry." Seeing the disappointment on Maria's face, Grandma added, "But I'll ask around. Maybe John remembers it."

Chris knew Grandma was talking about her brother, John Archer. He also knew that the next day she and Grandpa were going to be leaving to visit Uncle John in Seattle, Washington, for the week. "So you'll ask Uncle John if he remembers the picture?" Chris asked.

"Yes," Maria chimed in. "And if he has it, could you mail it to us? I think it might be a clue."

"A clue to what?" Grandma asked. "The combination to the safe?"

Maria and Chris looked at each other. Maria shook her head slightly. "I'm sorry, Grandma. We can't say for sure right now. We're working on solving an important mystery."

Two cars pulled into the driveway at nearly the same time. Chris looked out the window. "Grandpa's home," he announced. "And Mom and Dad are here to pick us up."

"OK. I'll go wake Yoyo up," Maria said. Yoyo was still rubbing her eyes when Mom and Dad and Grandpa walked into the kitchen through the back door.

"Well, hi, sleepyhead," Grandpa said, picking Yoyo up and giving her a kiss on the cheek. Yoyo finished rubbing her eyes and smiled at Mom and Dad. Grandpa handed her over to Dad.

"Did you have a nice date?" Maria asked Mom with a giggle.

Mom smiled. "We sure did. How was your evening at Grandma's?"

"Great," Chris and Maria said in unison.

"Maria and I won hide-and-seek," Yoyo said.

"Then she went to sleep," Chris added.

Before leaving for home, everyone gave

Grandma and Grandpa a big hug goodbye and wished them a safe flight. Grandma remembered the box of clothes and had Dad carry it out to the car so he could take it to church next week.

"Don't forget to ask Uncle John about the photograph," Maria reminded Grandma.

"I won't," Grandma assured her. "I'll ask him first thing."

When Dad stopped at an intersection on the way home, Chris looked up at the hill where the cross stood. Glowing in the lights that shone on it, the cross made him feel happy that he was a Christian. He wondered how many people thought about what Jesus did for them by dying on the cross.

Chris leaned over Yoyo so he could whisper to Maria. "Since we have to wait to see if Uncle John has that photograph you're looking for, let's work on finding the combination to Great-Grandpa's old safe. Maybe there's a clue in there that will help us prove Great-Grandpa donated the money for the cross."

Maria nodded her head. "OK."

Then Chris placed his finger in front of his lips and shook his head to tell Yoyo not to say anything.

Yoyo whispered, "OK."

Chris awoke with a start. "Wow! What a weird dream," he said to himself. "What a weird night of dreams." All night, he had been dreaming about the safe. He jumped out of bed and headed to Maria's room. "Maria, wake up!" He shook her until she stirred awake.

"What is it?" Maria asked sleepily.

Chris sat down on the floor with his back leaning against Maria's bed. "I've been tossing and turning all night, dreaming about the safe."

Maria turned her table lamp on. "What did you dream about it?"

"I dreamed we never found the combination. We looked everywhere too."

"Well, we haven't even started looking for the combination yet," Maria pointed out. "I don't think your dream is going to help us much, either."

Chris shrugged. "I guess not." After eating breakfast and getting ready for school, he found himself at his desk, holding the statue again. As he studied it carefully, a sound told him someone was watching him from the doorway of his bedroom.

"What are you doing, Chris?" Maria asked as

she stuck her head in the room.

"Just looking at the statue. It's neat to have something of Great-Grandpa's. It sort of helps me know him better," Chris said.

When school was finally over on Friday, Chris grabbed Maria by the arm just as they got outside and pulled her toward the car. "Come on, sis!"

"Why are you in such a hurry?" Maria asked.

"Maybe Grandma sent us that photograph you wanted. I've got a feeling she did, and it's waiting in the mailbox!"

"Let's go, then!" Maria said, and raced Chris to the car.

They both reached the car at the same time and tried to hop in the back seat, but Mom had three big bags of groceries sitting in the back seat too. Chris pushed the bags so he could get in. On the other side of the car, Maria yelled, "I've got to get in too, Chris!"

Chris tried adjusting the bags so both he and Maria could get in at the same time. Finally, they were both able to get inside and close the door.

When Chris looked up and told Mom they were ready to go, Yoyo was peering over the front seat at him and laughing.

"Buckle your seat belts," Mom said before she started the car.

At home, Chris hefted the last bag of groceries onto the kitchen counter and shrugged out of his jacket. Yoyo was dragging a carton of milk across the kitchen floor.

"Is that the last bag, Chris?" Mom asked.

Chris glanced at it and nodded. "Yup."

"Good. Thank you for bringing those in for me," Mom said. She leaned against the counter for a second. "Maria, please put the groceries away for me."

Maria started taking groceries out of the bags and putting them in the cupboards while Mom picked out the laundry soap and stain remover she had bought and headed to the laundry room. Chris started to go upstairs to make sure Yoyo hadn't messed with his statue, when Maria grabbed his arm.

"Oh no you don't! You've got to stay and help me put these groceries away!" she said.

"No, you have to put them away. I brought them inside," Chris retorted.

Maria made a face. She was just about to argue, when a voice in the living room started talking about *their* mystery!

5

Great-Grandpa Archer

Chris's mouth fell open. Maria's eyes got really big. *Who was Yoyo telling about their mystery?* Chris wondered.

They both ran into the living room.

"Yoyo! You were supposed to keep the mystery a secret!" Chris said.

"But I just told Teddy!" Yoyo whimpered as she hugged her stuffed bear. "Teddy can keep secrets. I'm sorry, Chwis."

"What are you all talking about?" Mom's firm voice said from the kitchen. Mom was standing behind them with her arms folded.

Chris's shoulders fell. *Now Mom will know about the safe too! I'd better explain it all so she understands why it's important.*

"Over at Grandma and Grandpa's last night, we found Great-Grandpa Archer's old safe when we were playing hide-and-seek," Chris explained. "Grandma told us no one knew what the combination to the old safe was, so it had never been opened. She said we could look through Great-Grandpa's old things that were in boxes beside the safe."

"I see," Mom said. "And what did you find?"

Chris lowered his eyes. "Nothing. Except I did find an old statue someone carved for Great-Grandpa. Grandma said I could keep it."

"And I found a bunch of old photographs," Maria added. "I told Chris I thought Great-Grandpa might be the one who donated the money for Mill Valley's cross on the hill. But I can't prove it. I remember a picture of Great-Grandpa standing beside the cross when he wasn't wearing a beard. I think it might be a clue. Grandma might send me a picture if she finds the one I remember at Uncle John's."

"I'll go get the statue for you to look at, Mom," Chris said. He got up and went to his room.

When he brought it out, Mom held out her hands for it.

"I remember this," Mom said. "It used to sit in your great-grandpa's study." She held it out and looked at it at different angles. "The man who carved this did a wonderful job. You'll have to take very good care of this, Chris."

Chris nodded. "I will."

Then Mrs. Vargas got quiet. Chris could tell by the look on her face that she was thinking about something. "I remember something else," she finally said. "Your great-grandpa kept a safe in his study too. It sat beside the big desk he used to write at. I also remember that one wall was filled with shelves full of books."

Chris went back to his room to get his note-book and pencil. When he got back, he wrote down Mom's description of Great-Grandpa's study. "How many books did Great-Grandpa write?" he asked.

"Thirty or forty, I believe."

"Forty books! Wow!" Chris exclaimed. He wrote that down too. "There's a lot more to this mystery than I thought."

"Should we tell the other Shoebox Kids?" Maria asked. "We might need their help, and the more heads the better if we're going to search for the combination to that safe."

"That's a good idea," Chris agreed.

"It sounds like you two have a lot of detective work to do," Mom said. She checked her watch. "It's been a long time since either of you saw Great-Grandpa's old house. If we can get the house ready for Sabbath quickly enough, maybe we should drive by and see it."

"I remember it from a long time ago," Maria said. "It's sort of scary looking."

"Do you think we might find the combination there?" Chris asked Mom.

"I don't know, Chris. It's a good idea to look everywhere, don't you think? People hide things in very peculiar places. I knew a woman who kept the combination to her safe in the phone book."

"Maybe Great-Grandpa wrote it on one of the bookshelves or something," Chris suggested.

Mom agreed. She sighed. "I wish the place had not been allowed to run down so much."

"What happened to it?" Chris wanted to know. "Why doesn't anyone live there anymore?"

Mom's eyebrows knitted together. "Well,"

she said, "I believe that when Grandpa Archer died, his belongings were divided equally among his children. The house was sold to pay off what was owed on it, and what was left over was divided up. None of his children could keep the house because it was so big and so expensive."

Maria slowly set a can of beans in the pantry while she listened to Mom. "What happened to the other owners?" she asked.

"The people who bought it lived there for several years and then sold it. The second set of owners had some financial problems, and the bank took the house back because they couldn't make the payments. It's just too big for most people. Now it's too run-down to attract buyers. If anyone were to buy it, they would have to make major repairs to it before moving in."

"Who owns it now?" Maria wanted to know.

"The city."

"Mill Valley owns Great-Grandpa Archer's house?"

"Yes, it does. Don't you remember a couple of years ago when I told your father that the city wanted to make it into a museum. It's in a good location. Not too far from downtown and in a historical section of town." Mrs. Vargas suddenly stood up and clapped her hands together. "Listen, guys, if we're going to go, we had better hurry and get the house clean. Maria, you can start on one bathroom while Chris cleans his room."

Chris went through his room like a tornado, picking up everything off the floor and bed. Somehow things got placed back in order, and the bed even got made in the process.

Maria cleaned the bathroom she was responsible for, and on her way past Chris's room handed the cleaning supplies off to him. He headed straight to the bathroom it was his duty to clean and started working.

When they had finished cleaning, they went downstairs and grabbed their jackets.

"Ready, Mom?" Chris called.

"Just a minute. I'm just finishing putting together a bean casserole for potluck tomorrow."

A moment later, Mrs. Vargas was slipping an arm into her jacket and reaching for her purse at the same time. She glanced outside. "I wish the wind would stop blowing. But I guess early spring is just a windy time of year. Let's hurry and go so we can be back before Dad gets home from work."

6

A Clue in the Mail

Great-Grandpa Archer's old house sat in the oldest section of Mill Valley. *The old house looks so strange here with those big business buildings just across the street*, Chris thought as he stared back through the old oak trees.

Mrs. Vargas pulled the car up to the curb and switched off the ignition. They sat in the car and just looked. "It must have been pretty once," Maria commented. Mom nodded.

Chris noticed that one of the windows on the second story was broken. Some vines were winding their way up the two columns that led to the

49

front door, and much of the paint was peeling. Worst of all, the house looked cold and dark. It certainly didn't look like a home.

Chris sat back in the seat and stared for a long time at Great-Grandpa's house. He tried to think about where Great-Grandpa would have hidden the combination to his safe and if Great-Grandpa was the one who donated the money to have the cross built. "Mom, do you think we can get inside the house and look around?" he asked.

Mom thought a minute. "Maybe. I'll ask the pastor to speak to the mayor about it. I don't see why we couldn't."

Chris hoped it would be all right. They needed to look inside Great-Grandpa's old house if they were going to have a chance of finding the combination. He was trying to fit the image of the house in his mind before Mom pulled away, when he saw something he hadn't noticed before. It was on the very top of the house. "Mom, what is that on the peak of the house?"

Mrs. Vargas leaned over and looked up through Maria's window. "That's a wind vane. It shows which way the wind is blowing."

"I know that, Mom. But it looks like a man shooting an arrow," Chris added. "It looks just like my statue!"

Dad was already home when Mom, Chris, Maria, and Yoyo came through the back door. He was sitting in his favorite chair reading the paper. "Where have you guys been?" Dad asked.

Maria opened the closet to put her jacket away. "We went to see Great-Grandpa Archer's old house."

Mom walked into the living room. "Chris is trying to find the combination to Grandpa Archer's old safe, and Maria is trying to prove Grandpa Archer donated the money for the cross up on the hill," she explained.

"Is that so?" Dad said. "Well, the paper has some news in it about the cross. It says someone has already claimed to have donated the money."

"I don't believe it!" Maria protested. "What if Chris and I prove Great-Grandpa was the one who donated the money for the cross?"

"Then Mill Valley will want to honor him for it," Dad said. "But you'll have to prove it."

"Well, that's what we're going to do," Maria stated.

Dad smiled. "I hope so. By the way, Maria, there is a letter addressed to you on the kitchen counter."

Chris thought Maria was going to trample him on her way to the kitchen. "I told you it was going to come today," he called after her.

Maria didn't open the letter as soon as she got it, like Chris would have. Instead, she started toward her room. "Are you coming, Chris?" she asked, cocking her head to one side. He was right behind her.

"I don't know if I want to open it," Maria said when they were settled on the floor next to her bed. "It might not be a clue like I was hoping for at all."

Chris smiled. "We have to look everywhere, remember? Real detectives don't always find a clue the first time. They make a lot of mistakes. Hurry, let's open it!"

Maria turned the envelope over and tore the flap open with her fingernail. She took out a piece of stationery with Grandma's handwriting on it. It read:

Dear Maria,
I hope this photograph is what you were looking for. It didn't take Uncle John long to find it. Good luck!
Love, Grandma

Maria took the photograph out of the envelope.

"You were right!" Chris exclaimed.

At the Shoebox the next morning, DeeDee stopped Chris. "Is Ryan coming today?"

Chris's friend, Ryan, often visited the Shoebox for church, even though he wasn't really a Christian. Chris shook his head. "No, he didn't want to come today."

"You know, I think Ryan isn't sure what he wants to do," Jenny said when she found out Ryan wasn't coming to church. She was sitting in a circle with the other Shoebox Kids.

DeeDee flipped her head back to get the hair out of her eyes. "I think he's annoying."

No one said a word, but DeeDee got a message from everyone's glares.

"OK, OK, maybe not annoying. But he always says Christians are crazy or dumb. Just when I think we've made him change his mind, he does or says something that makes me wonder why I even want to be his friend."

Chris felt his neck getting warm and wondered if it was turning red. Ryan was his friend, so he should at least say something in his defense. Suddenly he had an idea. "The disciples weren't the best followers of Jesus at first, either. Jesus had to be their friend for a long time before they changed their attitudes." Now all the Shoebox Kids were looking at him. So was Mrs. Shue.

"Look at Peter," Chris added, shrugging his shoulders. "Peter swore he didn't even know Jesus, and after all the love Jesus had shown him too."

"I think Chris has made a very good point," Mrs. Shue said.

"I guess so," DeeDee admitted. Sammy, Willie, and Jenny all agreed.

Later, while the class was working on its lesson, DeeDee came over and sat down next to Chris. "I'm sorry for what I said about Ryan. I'll to try to be more patient."

"Thank you," Chris replied. "Sometimes I don't know how to act or what to say around Ryan, either. But he is my . . . our friend."

Mrs. Shue looked at her watch. Then she stood up in front of the class. "Time really has gone quickly this morning. The other classes are probably out by now. Willie, will you have closing prayer?"

Willie nodded and maneuvered his wheel-chair into the circle as everyone bowed their heads.

Afterward, Mrs. Shue spoke again. "Remember, this afternoon after potluck, we are going for a hike. Mr. Shue is going to take us. DeeDee's parents and Pastor Hill are going too."

"I think my mom and dad are going," Maria said.

"Good," Mrs. Shue said. "See you all there."

Even though a cool breeze was blowing, people were outside visiting in small groups after church. Chris put his Bible away in the car and was headed back to the church, when Sammy caught up to him. "Maybe we should invite Ryan to go on the hike with us," Sammy suggested.

"Yeah, I think so too," Chris replied. "I'll go find Mom and Dad and see if they'll pick Ryan up if he wants to go with us."

Chris went inside and found Mom helping to fix potluck dinner. Mr. Vargas and Sammy Tan's grandfather were setting up tables. "Good idea, Chris," his mom agreed. "I'm sure your dad will pick Ryan up if he wants to go."

Dad winked at Chris. "No problem, Chris.

You go ahead and call Ryan and let me know if he wants to go."

Chris dialed Ryan's number while the other Shoebox Kids waited behind him. "May I speak to Ryan, please?" he asked when Ryan's mom answered the phone. He could hear Ryan being called to the phone, and then Ryan picked up the receiver.

"Hello?" Ryan said.

"Ryan, this is Chris. Maria, Jenny, Willie, Sammy, DeeDee, and I were wondering if you would like to come with us on a hike this afternoon. Do you think you could come?"

"Well, I—I don't know. I'd have to ask."

"It'll be fun," Chris put in.

"OK, I'll go ask." Ryan put down the receiver.

Chris cupped his hand over the mouthpiece while he waited. "What'd he say?" Jenny wanted to know.

"He's asking," Chris whispered.

A few seconds later, Ryan was back on the phone. "I can go!"

"Great! Dad and I will be there soon to pick you up."

7

Trail to Mill Valley Cross

The Tellers' big brown van pulled to a stop about two miles outside of Mill Valley near a sign that said Trail to Mill Valley Cross. The Shoebox Kids piled out into the parking lot.

Mr. Shue gathered everyone together before the hike and asked Jesus for protection and thanked Him for the beauty of nature. "The hike to the cross takes about an hour," he told the group. "But we're in no hurry, so let's stick together and enjoy the walk."

"It's been a long time since I was on this trail," Chris said. "Isn't it just a long dirt trail to the top? That could be tough for you, Willie."

Willie's eyes twinkled. "Wait until you see this!" He led the group around the van so they could see a long paved ramp leading down the hill toward the trail marker.

"Wow!" Chris exclaimed. "When did they do that?"

Willie popped his chair back on two wheels and laughed. "The city just finished it last week. And from the bottom there, a paved trail leads all the way up to the cross on the hill. Mr. Shue read about it in the paper. That's why we came here today."

"Wow," Sammy Tan said. "We're going to have to bring our bikes here this summer."

"It's pretty neat if you ask me," Willie said.

"It's great!" Jenny added.

Willie turned around and headed toward the ramp. "Let's go! I'll race you to the trail marker!"

"Don't we have to wait for Mr. Shue?" Jenny asked. But it was too late.

Before anyone could even move, Willie started down the ramp. He turned to give everyone a quick grin before twisting his head back to see what he was doing. Suddenly his left hand slipped, and the wheelchair swung to the right.

Then the right wheel slid off the ramp!

"He's going to crash!" DeeDee yelled.

Willie managed to get both wheels on the ramp again, but by now he was going way too fast. For a second, everyone just stood there and stared.

Then Maria grabbed Chris's arm and yanked him forward as she started skipping sideways down the hill. "Come on! We'll cut him off!" Chris almost tripped, but he managed to stay on his feet, moving downhill as fast as he could go without falling.

Sammy, Jenny, and DeeDee were right behind. "Hang on, Willie!" DeeDee shouted. Willie's eyes were as big as Mrs. Shue's sugar cookies as he raced down the ramp. It took all his skill as a driver to keep his wheelchair on the ramp and keep it from flipping over.

Ryan didn't even try skipping sideways down the steep hill. He ran straight down and started going faster and faster and faster. Before he could do anything about it, his head and shoulders were going faster than his feet could go.

"Ryan looks like he's going to fly," Maria shouted to Chris.

Chris leapt over a bush. "If he does, he won't

stay up very long."

At least Ryan is getting down the hill faster than anyone else. In about two seconds, Chris realized, *Ryan is going to hit the ramp right behind Willie's speeding wheelchair. If anyone could stop Willie, it would have to be Ryan!*

Suddenly, Ryan's feet hit the ramp. As he started to tumble over, he grabbed the handles on Willie's chair and hung on.

"Slow me down, Ryan!" Willie yelled.

Amazingly, Ryan held on as the chair dragged him. A few seconds later, Chris and Maria were close enough to grab onto Willie's wheelchair and pull it to a stop.

"Wow!" DeeDee said as she arrived. "I thought you were a goner, Willie."

Willie ran an arm across his forehead. "So did I, DeeDee. Thanks to Ryan, I didn't have to try going around that last corner. I wouldn't have made it."

After shouting back to the adults that everyone was OK, the Shoebox Kids walked slowly on down to the corner by the trail marker. "You're right," Chris said to Willie. "You never would have made it." He turned to Ryan. "You were great. The way you blasted down that hill to catch Willie, I thought you were going to fly."

"Yeah, thanks, Ryan," Willie added. "There would have been an awful crash if you hadn't stopped me in time."

Ryan had a sheepish look on his face. "I—I really didn't do much."

"Sure you did!" DeeDee said. "You saved Willie's life."

"Ah, don't be so dramatic. I just got going so fast I couldn't stop until I got to the ramp," Ryan explained. "I honestly—"

"Save it," Chris said, winking at Ryan. "You did a great job. Don't try to pretend you didn't." *I'm sure Ryan grabbed Willie's chair so he wouldn't fall over. I guess no one else noticed that. But he was running down the hill to help Willie just like the rest of us.*

When the grown-ups got to the bottom of the hill, Mr. Shue studied the Shoebox Kids through narrow eyes. "Are you all right, Willie?"

"Yes, sir," Willie answered.

"Good. That's very good." But Mr. Shue didn't lose the troubled look. "Next time, it might be wise to come down the hill a bit more slowly."

"Yes, Mr. Shue, we will," the Shoebox Kids replied in unison.

Maria gave Chris a sharp nudge in the side. Then she leaned over and whispered into his ear. Chris cleared his throat "Um . . . can we go on ahead of the rest of the group?" Chris asked.

Mr. Shue rubbed his chin for a moment. He usually rubbed his chin before he answered a "can we" question. "If you don't get too far ahead," he said. "When you get to the cross, wait for the rest of us slow people. OK?"

Chris and Maria waited until they were out of sight of the grown-ups before calling the Shoebox Kids together to tell them about the mystery. Everyone gathered around Willie and kept walking. "We have another mystery to solve," Chris said secretively. "Maria and I decided we need your help to solve it."

"Great!" Jenny said. Then she frowned. "It's not someone's pet disappearing again, is it?"

"No, not that," Chris answered. As everyone gathered, Chris noticed that Ryan was pushing Willie's wheelchair. *Willie never lets anyone push his wheelchair. And DeeDee is walking right beside Ryan like he's her best friend.* Suddenly, he was jealous of Ryan.

Maria got tired of waiting for Chris to explain the mystery. "When we were playing down in Grandma and Grandpa's basement, we found an old safe that belonged to our Great-Grandpa Archer. It hasn't been opened for years, because no one knows what the combination is. Grandma said we could open it if we found it."

Chris finally spoke up. "And Maria thinks we might be able to prove that Great-Grandpa Archer is the one who donated the money for the cross up here."

"That sounds interesting," DeeDee said. "Doesn't it, Ryan?"

"Yeah, it does!" Ryan said. "Hey, maybe there's some evidence in the safe that proves your great-grandpa really did donate the cross."

"That's what Maria and I thought," Chris agreed.

Willie frowned. "Do you know where to look? I mean, the combination could be anywhere."

"That's the whole point of solving the mystery." Chris sighed.

"Right," Willie said. "I forgot."

"Hey," Ryan said suddenly, "let's hurry and get to the cross!"

"OK," Willie said. "Let's go!"

Chris started to run with everybody else, when he felt a sharp pain in his foot. "Ouch!" he cried as he stopped. Everyone else kept going as he untied his shoe. *I must have gotten a rock in my shoe when I was coming down the side of that hill. It sure hurts!* Sitting down beside the trail, he took off his shoe and emptied a small rock out onto the trail.

When Chris finally got to the cross, where everyone was supposed to meet, he caught a glimpse of DeeDee's yellow jacket disappearing around the next corner. "Hey, wait up, guys!" he yelled.

He ran around the same corner. "Hey . . . guys—" He choked on his words. He was all alone! He stopped in his tracks and frowned. Where had everyone gone?

8

A Dirty Trick

Chris scanned the brush and trees on his right. Then he looked up the hill on his left. "OK, guys. I know you're around here somewhere."

No one answered.

Maybe I didn't see DeeDee's yellow jacket after all, Chris thought. *Maybe they're even farther ahead somewhere.* Chris took off jogging. He jogged for five more minutes before stopping to catch his breath. *Where could they have gone?*

He could see a long way down the trail, but he couldn't see his friends. *I'd better go back and tell Mr. Shue I can't find them*, he thought. Turning around, Chris started running back up the trail. *How am I going to explain this?*

But when he got back to the cross, Chris didn't have to explain anything. Everyone, including Ryan and the other Shoebox Kids, was standing around the cross.

Chris slowed to a walk, breathing hard after all the running he had done. "What happened to you?" Sammy asked, trying to hide a grin.

"Yeah," Ryan added. "What happened?"

"I went down the trail to see if I could find you guys. Where were you?"

Then Mr. Shue and Mr. and Mrs. Vargas walked over, and Chris knew he was in some sort of trouble. Dad spoke first. "Chris, your mom and I were getting worried. Mr. Shue was also very worried. Do you mind explaining why you decided to take off on your own and get so far ahead of the group?"

"I wasn't . . . I mean, I didn't . . ." Chris didn't know what to say.

Willie rolled his wheelchair forward. He put his head down but still managed to look at the Vargases and Mr. Shue. "It was our fault. We got too far ahead, and when Chris came to find us, we hid from him. Then we circled around and got back here before he did."

Mr. Shue doesn't look too pleased, but at least he's not mad at me, Chris thought. Just then, Pastor Hill came up. "I spoke to the mayor Friday afternoon, Chris, right after your mom called. The mayor said there would be no problem letting you inside your great-grandpa's old house to look around as long as there was an adult along."

"Great!" Chris said. "Thanks." He turned to tell the others, but then he remembered what they had done to him. *Let them find their own mystery to solve*, he decided.

Chris slept in late on Sunday morning. But he heard Maria coming before she opened his door and shouted, "Hey, wake up. It's time for breakfast."

He just rolled over. "I don't feel like eating. Just go away."

Maria stared for a minute, then shrugged her shoulders. "I'll tell Mom you're sick."

That made Chris sit up. "No! Don't tell Mom. She'll just make me take some yucky medicine."

"But if you're sick—"

"I didn't say I was sick. I just don't feel like

eating," Chris interrupted.

"Then you have to be sick," Maria declared. She tried one more time. "We're having pancakes."

"Go ahead and eat. I just don't feel like it."

Chris heard Mom come up the stairs. Then he heard Maria tell her that he didn't feel well, but that he wasn't sick, either. He could imagine Maria shrugging her shoulders. Mom didn't come in his room, and he was glad about that. *I can't explain why I don't feel good. I just don't.*

At ten-thirty, Chris finally crawled out of bed and took a shower. When he got downstairs, Maria claimed Ryan had called.

"I never heard the phone," Chris said as he got a box of cereal out of the cupboard.

"You must have been in the shower," Maria said. "Anyway, he wants us to all meet over here at noon so we can work on the case."

"What case?"

Maria rolled her eyes. "Our case, Mr. Detective! We've got to find the combination to the safe and prove Great-Grandpa Archer is the one who donated the money for the cross. Next Thursday is the day the town is going to honor somebody for it. We have to make sure they honor the right person."

"I wish you'd stop rolling your eyes, Maria. One of these days they're going to stick halfway." Chris slumped down at the table. "Let Ryan find the missing combination. Everyone seems to like Ryan better than me, anyway. In Mrs. Shue's class yesterday, I was the only one who would stick up for him. But after he saved Willie, everyone decided that he's the greatest."

Chris poured milk on his cereal. Maria wasn't helping matters any by rolling her eyes.

"Is that what's been bothering you?" Maria asked. "You're jealous?"

"I'm not either."

"You're jealous of Ryan. Face it," Maria said.

Chris knew Maria was right. *She didn't have to rub it in, though*. There was no way to argue with her, so he got the biggest spoonful of cereal and milk he could get on his spoon and stuck it in his mouth.

By noon, Maria's rolling eyes were beginning to get on Chris's nerves. He grabbed his notebook and went into the family room, where it was quiet. *Maria can answer the door when everyone gets here*, he thought.

At noon, the doorbell rang for the first time.

Chris could hear Jenny's and DeeDee's voices in the living room. Then the doorbell rang again. He heard Dad helping Willie Teller get his wheelchair up the steps. Finally, he decided to join everyone in the living room.

"Is Ryan here?" he asked when he entered the living room.

"No," Maria replied.

"Hi, Chris," Willie said. "You're not still sore about the trick we pulled on you yesterday, are you?"

Chris shook his head. "Naw, I guess not."

"Good," Willie said. "Ryan felt bad afterward."

"He did?" Chris asked

"Yeah. He said it wasn't a very nice thing to do, especially to a friend," Willie said.

Just then, the doorbell rang again. This time, it was Sammy and Ryan.

"Hi, everyone," Sammy said when he came inside.

Ryan just waved. He tried to avoid Chris's eyes. Chris didn't say anything, either.

Suddenly, Willie couldn't stand it any longer. He rolled his wheelchair to the middle of the room. "What is it with you two?" he asked Chris and

Ryan. "You two were best friends until yesterday. It wasn't very nice of us to pull that disappearing trick on you, Chris, but it wasn't all Ryan's fault. We're all sorry. Will you forgive us?"

Jenny stood up. She acted like she was going to say something, but then she sat down again.

Chris stood up. "I'm sorry I acted jealous, Ryan. I guess I was just jealous because everyone was hanging around you. I think it's great you're part of the group, but I guess that means I've got to share you with my other friends too."

Ryan grinned. "I'm sorry too, Chris. I really like being around all you guys."

Jenny stood up again. "Now that that's all settled," she said, "can we get on with solving this mystery?"

"OK," Chris said. "Everyone gather around. Maria has an idea."

Maria laid out her photographs on the floor. She only needed three to prove her point. "When Chris, Yoyo, and I were playing hide-and-seek in Grandma's basement last Sunday, we found an old safe of our Great-Grandpa Archer's. That's Grandma's dad," Maria explained.

The Shoebox Kids nodded.

"Well, Grandma told Chris and I that we

could look through some of Great-Grandpa's old things."

"Great-Grandpa died almost twenty years ago," Chris added.

Sammy, Jenny, DeeDee, and Ryan all knelt down close to the photographs.

Maria went on. "Most of the photographs we found when we were going through Great-Grandpa's things had dates on the back of them. Mom puts dates on the backs of our photos too. So does Grandma."

"My mom does that too," Willie said.

"Most people do," Chris said.

"In all the photos of Great-Grandpa Archer," Maria continued, "he was wearing a beard. But I saw a photo of him one time where he wasn't wearing a beard. I knew it was somewhere, but I didn't know where. I also remembered he was standing beside the cross that we hiked to yesterday, the one the city is planning a fiftieth-anniversary celebration for this week."

"What does that prove?" Ryan asked.

"It doesn't really prove anything," Maria said. "But the photograph I got from Grandma last Friday shows Great-Grandpa without a beard. The date on it was fifty years ago. See?" Maria held the photograph up for everyone to see.

"Wait," Willie said. "I can't read what else it says."

"That's the best part," Maria said. "The writing on the back of the photograph says 'Miles Archer and Mayor Bill Parker 1945.' I can also prove the photo was taken close to fifty years ago because of these other two photographs. The one where Great-Grandpa has a full beard is dated 1944, and the one where he's just starting to grow a beard is dated 1945. Grandma said she only remembered one time when he didn't wear a beard."

"So you think your great-grandpa is the one who donated the money for the cross on the hill?" Sammy asked.

Chris and Maria both nodded.

"But we still have to prove it," Ryan said.

"That's where another part of the mystery comes in," Chris said. "The part about the missing combination to Great-Grandpa's old safe. Hopefully something is inside that will help prove Great-Grandpa is the one who donated the money for the cross." He grinned. "And here's the best part. Mom said she would take us to Great-Grandpa's house. Right now!"

9

Great-Grandpa Archer's Old House

At just that moment, Mrs. Vargas opened the front door. "Is everyone ready to search for clues?" she asked.

"Yes!"

Chris started to run out the door with the rest of the Shoebox Kids, when he remembered his backpack. He hurried back inside and grabbed it from beside the front door. *We might need the flashlight. And I always need my notebook and pencil.* He grabbed the statue of the archer, too, so he could show it to everyone.

Maria and Chris climbed into the van next to

Willie. Behind them, Jenny and DeeDee and Sammy and Ryan were taking up the back seat and making a lot of noise. Chris took the archer out of his backpack and passed it back to Ryan and Sammy.

"Wow! This is great!" Ryan said. He touched his finger to the tip of the arrow. "It's not very sharp."

DeeDee sighed. "Does everything have to be dangerous for boys to like it? Let me see it, Ryan."

Ryan passed the statue along to DeeDee. She frowned as she stared at it. "I think he's ugly," she decided.

"Does everything have to be cute for girls to like it?" Ryan teased.

Ten minutes later, Mom drove slowly past the house while the Shoebox Kids pressed their noses against the driver's side windows. "I'm going to pull into a parking lot up here and turn around so when we park we won't have to cross the street," Mom said.

"That sure is a big house," DeeDee commented.

"Yeah," Sammy agreed. "Are you sure we can go inside?"

Mom jingled a set of keys together. "Here's

our ticket," she said. "Pastor Hill borrowed these from the mayor just for us."

"I'm not so sure I want to go in," Jenny said as they pulled up in front of the old house. "It looks scary." For a minute, everyone sat very still. And quiet.

Then Ryan spoke up. "Come on. Let's go."

Mrs. Vargas led them up to the front door and unlocked it. She opened the door, but let the Shoebox Kids go inside to the living room by themselves. "Remember, this house belongs to the city. Don't disturb anything. If you need me, I'll be walking around outside, remembering this old house, Chris."

"All right, Mom," Chris replied. He turned to the Shoebox Kids. "Let's go search for the combination."

"Wow, this house is *big*," Jenny said. "I wish my house was this big. I could have three rooms of my own."

"You wouldn't like it for very long," Sammy and Willie said at the same time. They both laughed. "You'd get tired of cleaning it."

Jenny looked around again. The place was very dusty. "Yeah, I guess so. I didn't think of it that way."

"Where should we look for this combination?" DeeDee asked. "Are there any papers or boxes of stuff to look through?"

"Not that we know of," Chris answered. "The only things left here are the walls and the furniture."

Chris walked out into the middle of the living room. "I don't think this is the best place. There doesn't seem to be anywhere to write a combination that the other owners would not have discovered or covered up somehow."

"What if he scratched the numbers of the combination into some woodwork somewhere with a knife?" Ryan asked.

"I don't think so," Willie answered. "You know how adults hate it when someone scratches on a desk or table."

"It was just an idea," Ryan said, shrugging.

"It was a good idea," Chris said. "If we just knew where to look."

Maria walked over to the bottom of the stairs and looked up. "I think the best place to look would be where Great-Grandpa's study was. Where Mom said the safe was."

"Right!" the Shoebox Kids agreed. "Let's go!"

Willie rolled over and looked at the long

flight of stairs. "It won't take all of us to search one room. You guys go ahead."

Chris slid off his backpack and pulled out his flashlight. Then he handed the backpack to Willie. "Can you hang onto this?"

"Sure," Willie said.

At the top of the stairs, after waving down to Willie, everyone spread out to look for Great-Grandpa Archer's study. "It's the room with lots of bookshelves," Chris reminded them.

Maria opened a door and peered inside. "This isn't it," she said.

Sammy and Jenny didn't find it, either, in the two rooms they looked in.

Chris went to the far end of the hall and slowly opened a door. "Hey, everyone, this looks like it!" It was a little darker inside than Chris hoped it would be. Turning his flashlight on, he stepped inside, shining the light back and forth. One whole wall was lined with bookshelves, just like Mom had said. Fancy woodwork crossed the edges of the ceiling and circled around the window.

"See anything?" Ryan asked as he dashed in.

"I haven't looked yet," Chris replied.

"Well, come on," Ryan said. He got ahead of

Chris and walked toward the bookshelves. Suddenly, he froze.

"What's the matter, Ryan?" Maria asked in a shaky voice.

"Spider webs! Pooh, phooey! Yuck. I hate spider webs," Ryan said. He started wiping the sticky webs off his face. Maria, Jenny, DeeDee, and Sammy all started giggling.

Ignoring them, Chris walked over to the window and looked outside. "Hey, Maria! Look at this!"

Maria ran over. "What is it?"

"You can see the cross perfectly from here. Great-Grandpa *must* have donated the money for it, maybe so he could see it whenever he looked out from his study."

"But it still doesn't prove anything," Maria said.

After the spider webs had partially been cleaned out from around the bookshelves, the Shoebox Kids searched every inch of the room. Chris, Maria, and Ryan even looked underneath the shelves as well as on tops of the shelves and at the wood around the windows. Ryan seemed to be most disappointed.

"If I wanted to hide a combination just in

case I forgot it, I'd carve it into the wood some-where," he said.

"I guess it's not here." Chris sighed. "After so long, who knows where it could be? Maybe it's lost forever."

Suddenly, Sammy ran to the door. "Did you hear that?" His face turned white. "I think Willie's in trouble!"

Just then, everyone heard Willie yell from downstairs!

10

The Missing Clue Wasn't Missing

Chris burst out of Great-Grandpa Archer's study, with Ryan, Sammy, DeeDee, Jenny, and Maria close behind him. He hurried down the stairs as fast as he could without running, just in case he might trip, and jumped the last two steps to the landing.

Willie was in the middle of the living room, and he looked really excited. He was holding the statue with both hands. "Come here, Chris!" he called. "And bring the flashlight."

Chris ran to Willie. "What's wrong?"

Willie didn't answer right away. He was too

excited. He just turned the statue over and pointed at the bottom of it. "Shine the light right there."

"OK," Chris said.

The Shoebox Kids all crowded around. "What are you doing?" Maria asked.

Chris shrugged. "I don't know. Willie must have found something."

"Hold the light still, Chris," Willie said. "Now, shine it at an angle."

"I think I see it!" Ryan exclaimed.

"Steady, Chris," Willie said again. "Yeah!"

Maria smiled. "I see it too! Do you see it, Chris?"

Chris couldn't believe his eyes. With the light shining at an angle like that, numbers appeared on the bottom of the statue. "The light is causing shadows," he said. "We couldn't see anything before because the numbers were too faint to see."

Chris suddenly realized that he'd been carrying the combination to the safe around with him and didn't even know it. He started laughing. "I've had it all along!" he said.

Just then, the door popped open. "Is everyone OK in here?" Mrs. Vargas asked.

Chris's smile was almost too big for his face. "Mom, you aren't going to believe this."

It didn't take long to convince Mom that they needed to go straight to Grandma and Grandpa's house. "I guess they won't mind if you kids go down to the basement to open the safe while they are gone. I need to feed Grandma's fish, anyway, so we'll just take care of everything at once," she said.

She opened the back door, and Chris led the way downstairs. Willie parked at the top of the stairs to wait.

Kneeling in front of the safe, Chris held up the statue. "Maria, hold the light still." He tilted the archer until he could see the numbers. Before he started to open it, he looked at the Shoebox Kids. "Maybe we should pray that it opens," he suggested.

Surprisingly, Ryan was the first one to agree. "That's a good idea," he said with a smile. "And let's pray for a neat treasure," he added.

Everyone bowed while Chris prayed. "Thank You, Jesus, for helping us find the combination to the safe. And please help it open. Amen."

Chris turned the dial to the first number—23—then the second number—14—then to the third number—30. Then he grabbed the handle and yanked it.

Nothing happened!

Chris's heart sank. "It doesn't work!"

"Wait a second," Willie called from the doorway. "Did you turn the dial correctly?"

"How many ways are there to open a safe?" Chris asked. He stood up and went back to where he could see Willie.

"There's only one right way," Willie said. "You've got to turn the dials the right way. First, clear it by turning it several times to the right. Now, go to the left until you get to the first number."

Chris raced back and knelt down again. "OK," he called when he hit number 23 again. "Now what?"

"Now, to the right, once all the way around until you get to the second number. Then go back to the left, all the way around until you get to the third number. Does it open?"

Chris turned the dial carefully, following Willie's instructions. Then he yanked on the handle again. This time, it turned easily.

As the door creaked open, DeeDee let out a long breath of air. "It doesn't look like there's anything inside but a few old papers."

Is that it? Chris wondered as he stared into the safe. *Is that the whole treasure?*

The next weekend at the Shoebox, Chris was carrying a thin white box. He set it on the table and sat down until class started. Just before Mrs. Shue had opening prayer, Ryan popped in the doorway.

"Surprise," he said.

He was greeted with smiles all around. "Hi, Ryan."

Mrs. Shue got up front and started class with prayer. Then she had an announcement. "This is a special occasion at the Shoebox," she said. "Chris and Maria, will you come up front and explain?"

Chris and Maria stood in front of the class. Maria opened the box and took out a big plaque and held it in her arms. Chris pointed to the polished wood as he began to explain.

"Since you all helped Maria and me prove that our Great-Grandpa Archer donated the money for the cross on the hill, we thought that the Shoebox would be the best place to hang the award the mayor gave to our family."

"How were you able to prove your great-grandpa was the one who helped build it?" Mrs. Shue asked.

"First of all, Maria remembered a fifty-year-old photograph of Great-Grandpa Archer standing with the mayor of Mill Valley. That helped us think he was the one who helped build it. Plus, when we were looking for clues in his old house, we discovered his study window had a great view of the cross. But none of that proved anything."

Ryan spoke up. "It's a good thing you found the combination to that safe."

Chris had to smile. "You mean it's a good thing Willie figured out that I had the combination all along. The treasure we found inside the safe was a letter."

Maria carefully unfolded an old piece of paper to show Mrs. Shue. "It's a thank-you note to Great-Grandpa Archer from the mayor of Mill Valley. See, the date shows that it was written fifty years ago."

"We accepted the plaque on behalf of our great-grandpa during the award ceremony," Chris said. "Thank you all for helping us find the combination and helping us honor our great-grandfather."

Maria passed the plaque around so all the Shoebox Kids could see it. It said, To Miles Archer, for helping the community of Mill Valley remember Jesus' love.